Kindred Verse

A Collection of Poems Inspired by *Anne of Green Gables*

By Julie A. Sellers

BLUE
CEDAR
PRESS

Blue Cedar Press
Wichita, Kansas

**BLUE
CEDAR
PRESS**

Blue Cedar Press
PO Box 48715
Wichita, KS 67201
bluecedarpress.com

First edition

Anne of Green Gables is a trademark of the Anne of Green Gables Licensing Authority Inc.

ISBN: 978-1-7342272-4-6
Photographs by Julie A. Sellers
Layout and design by Jay Wallace
Author photograph by Terrence Sims
Map used with permission of Alamy

Printed in the United States by IngramSpark and Amazon

For Mozzie

my canine kindred spirit

"Like-minded souls" walk the hallowed ground of the author's special places, catch glimpses of Anne in dunes, a bookcase, paths and blossoms, in reflections and possibility–a tonic for those who are "farsick for Green Gables."
—Mary Beth Cavert, L.M. Montgomery Institute Legacy Award (2020); publisher, *The Shining Scroll*

Sellers channels Anne's spirit as if she is Anne reincarnate and a remarkable friendship transcending time and location occurs. She goes looking for Anne and finds herself, a woman transformed by a fictional friend. A timeless, beautifully magical book.
—Ronda Miller, Author and Kansas Authors Club President (2018–2019)

Sellers deftly explores the intersecting spaces of memory, imagination, and life, wandering Anne-like through each. Inspiring future generations of writers as she was inspired, this book is the friend Sellers describes: "waiting to be discovered."
—Trinna S. Frever, L.M. Montgomery Scholar & Author

Sellers's dreamy words continue the legacy of Montgomery's heroine, creating another space for kindred spirits to connect with hope, beauty, and compassion, with Anne's impact on a Kansas girlhood, and with the transformative beauty of Prince Edward Island.
—Chloe Goodyear, Co-Producer "Annedemic: The East Pointers and Friends Read *Anne of Green Gables*"

Sellers writes: "Anne dreamed us all / into being," and gives us farsick, longing for places seen only through Anne's eyes. Montgomery's love of Prince Edward Island led Sellers to rediscover her own prairie landscape, "wind and stars and fireflies" and magic.
— Deirdre Kessler, former Prince Edward Island Poet Laureate

Using an array of poetic forms, Sellers captures the spirit of indomitable Anne Shirley with skill and insight. With "Gilbert Blythe," she portrays in seventeen words a pivotal moment in Anne's stormy relationship with Gilbert. Julie Sellers is a gifted writer.
—Duane R. Johnson, Poet & Kansas Author's Club President

Lifelong devotees of character Anne Shirley will find *Kindred Verse* essential reading. Readers who have never read *Anne of Green Gables* will also luxuriate in Sellers' metaphors. Sellers elucidates the longing we have to reread books we cherish; isn't that, after all, why we all read?
—Roy Beckemeyer, poet, author of *Mouth Brimming Over*

All of Anne's longtime "bosom friends"—and new ones!—will treasure this collection of verse. Sellers vividly recreates Anne's world with the living insight that can only come from a true kindred spirit. Prepare to be delightfully transported to Green Gables in each poem.
—Lesley Sieger-Walls, Ph.D., English

Dwell among this beautiful collection. If you've not read the series about the many-faceted Anne Shirley, this book is the perfect introduction. Julie Sellers' words remain with the reader long after turning the final page.
—Nancy Julien Kopp, author, blogger of *Writer Granny's World*

CONTENTS

Preface

I distinctly remember the day I made the acquaintance of Anne Shirley. It was a hot, June afternoon in Manhattan, Kansas, where I had been dragged along against my will on a college visit for my older sister. I was fourteen, and thoughts of college were still far from my mind. I only knew I was bored and had finished the novel I'd brought with me. My father decided to bribe me into silence in the best way he knew how: with more reading material.

"I'll buy you one book," he told me when we ended up in Varney's bookstore near the Kansas State University campus.

"Any book?" I asked, already honing my skills in questions of literary diplomacy.

Happy for the first time all day, I perused the aisles and considered my options. I had narrowed my choices down to two by the time my mother informed me we needed to leave, although I have no memory of what the other option was. I shudder to think that I almost didn't choose *Anne of Green Gables*, but I did. Clearly, destiny could not be thwarted.

The ninety-mile drive home probably convinced my father that his idea had been a stroke of genius, although in the years after that, he and my entire family might have questioned its advisability. He had placed in my hands the proof of a girl who, like myself, had an active imagination, love of nature, dreamed of writing, and could become so caught up in her reading and thoughts that she was oblivious to all else. Anne, despite any predictions to the contrary, had turned out just fine.

Both Anne's mishaps and her dreams endeared her to me, and I felt I would never overcome the lifelong sorrow of having my middle name spelled without the distinguished "e". Like Anne, I was often deemed impractical or scatterbrained, and my literary aspirations were mocked. But with Anne, I now knew I was not alone. If Anne existed and continued to exist in print after all those years, others must have identified with her, too, I reasoned, and I knew exactly who those people were: my kindred spirits. If a piece of literature could so succinctly portray who we were, then I, too, intended to share my own writing with the world.

Within a couple of years, I discovered my own bosom friend, Lesley, another devoted disciple of Anne Shirley. Lesley confirmed my belief that kindred spirits were real, for she understood my intertextual references, Anne-speak, and all my Anne-like hopes and dreams. We were positive the world must be full of like-minded souls, just waiting to be discovered. Time and experience have proven this to be true.

To know Anne is to love her and interact with her; passive reading is not an option because Anne was anything but a passive reader. She teaches us how to make our reading come alive and colors our own perceptions of snowy blossoms, shining waters, or the perfume of narcissi. Kindred spirits feel an intimate connection with Anne, and she is a part of each of us in unique ways.

This collection represents different facets of my decades-long friendship with Anne Shirley. May it encourage you to rethink your own relationship with Anne or to cultivate one if you do not yet know her. And above all, may it inspire you to dream as only those who belong to the race that knows Joseph can.

Julie A. Sellers
Atchison, Kansas

Kindred Spirits

You are there,
though I have never met you,
heart beating in time
with mine.
We meet
along the red dirt roads,
in Lover's Lane,
among the blossoms of Violet Vale,
and share a prickly thrill
in the shadows of the Haunted Wood.
We dream
of a bosom friend,
puffed sleeves,
winning the Avery,
a Matthew's faith in us,
and a Gilbert's devotion.
Anne dreamed us all
into being,
this community
of like-minded souls.
And you are there
waiting to be discovered
around the bend in the road,
across the miles and years,
with the turning of the page.

A Home for Imperfect Girls

I am farsick for Green Gables,
that perfect home
for an imperfect girl
that summons hearts
with its siren call
to kindred spirits
around the globe
and across the years.
And I feel keenly
this nostalgic longing
to be
in Lover's Lane or Violet Vale,
winding along the ruddy roads,
the White Way of Delight
a bower of dreams overhead.
The home lights, like fireflies,
beckon in the dusk.
The sea's longing whisper
accompanies my reverie.
And in the sweetness of the shadows
of woods and blooms and shore and lanes,
the heartbeat of imagination calls.
I glance over my shoulder,
looking for Green Gables,
for Anne,
for myself so many years ago,
imperfect girls
dreaming of
this perfect home.

Looking for Anne: Postcard from Prince Edward Island

I came looking for Anne Shirley, but I couldn't find her at Green Gables. Oh, they had paid careful attention to detail in that house with Bonny the geranium in the kitchen window, Marilla's amethyst brooch, Anne's much-coveted puffed sleeve dress, and the pieces of a broken slate, cracked emphatically over Gilbert's head. It was all very accurate to the fiction of the story, but somehow, none of it looked quite as I had imagined it as a girl, and in successive readings since. Anne, as my own fellowship with the novel had painted her, was nowhere to be found.

So, I went outside, and I wandered, following Lover's Lane, that woodsy path of solitude that had been much-loved by Anne's creator. The boughs, verdant and leafy, closed above me, and looking down the tunnel they shaped, I spied a shadowy form. Logic insisted it was just another tourist, but I held onto some strange hope that at last, I had spied Anne. I followed the path deeper into the trees, through lush ferns and wildflowers and over a tinkling brook, breathing deeply of the fresh stillness and landscapes that spoke of Anne. From there, I continued to the Haunted Wood, a spooky sensation crawling across my flesh as I relived Anne's fright there in the novel. I was positive I could glimpse her among the shadows.

With one last, backwards glance at Green Gables, I left the National Park and made my way to Cavendish Beach. A breeze tousled my hair as I followed the marked trail along the dunes. Birds sang beside the pond, and butterflies flitted among the wildflowers and wild roses. I could envision Anne picking a great bouquet of them, perhaps to adorn her hat or just to beautify the starkness of her east gable room. As I made my way to the shoreline, I paused to feel the sun on my face, the salty wind about me. There, before me, stretched the sands and red cliffs of the north shore, the intense blue of the sea sparkling beyond. The dunes rolled out before me, begowned in whispering grass. I breathed deeply of that natural landscape, of Anne's true home, exactly as I had always imagined it. As I slowly made my way to the beach, two shadows joined me: one, a red-headed heroine, the other, a long-ago version of myself. We walked there, in that iconic setting, in a literary communion that stretched across the years.

Hallowed Ground

"It is and ever must be hallowed ground to me."
—L.M. Montgomery of her home in Cavendish

If these old stones could speak in the tongues of dryads, they would distill their legend in the dappled breeze and whisper their story through the tangle of ferns filling the spaces between them. Roots reach down, parting the red soil of generations, nurturing themselves in all the truths and fictions lived and dreamed atop this foundation and in the fields beyond. A spark, the flash, a seed of vision, and Anne is born. Shadows play hide and seek with lustrous rays under the branches of the aged apple tree, and I, like Maud, know undeniably I am treading hallowed ground.

Talisman of Dreams

from summer footsteps
lacy petals rise and bloom
talisman of dreams

The Enchanted Bookcase

The polished glass
is a mirror of the soul
for all devoted pilgrims
who stand,
as I do now,
in reverence
before this altar of imagination.
I breathe the stillness,
see my eyes searching
the lustrous pane
for former writings of myself.
And in the flickering light,
I find all the faces
of all the girls
looking for Maud
looking for Anne
looking for Katie Maurice,
their dreams
reflected in
my own.

On Cavendish Beach

The song of the sea is salty in its mournful ebb and flow. The haunting call of gulls on the wind lulls me as I wander barefoot below, and on the dunes, the dry grass rings like chimes upon the breeze. The air is laced with sweet perfume from a nearby wild rose. White waters crash upon the crags and trip along the coast, and I ramble through the somnolent scene searching, seeking, scouring the shore for a glimpse of the immortal Anne. The waves embrace the paths we write across the years and sands.

A Sweet and Subtle Spell

"Remembrance wove a sweet and subtle spell…"
—*Anne of the Island*

My memories weave
a sweet and subtle spell
that conjures up an Eden
from the pages of the past.
Whispered zephyrs
flutter the leaves,
turn back the clock,
unravel a labyrinth of vines,
reveal golden perfumes,
dusky melodies,
and ambrosial dreams
envisioned upon a rustic bench.
We will meet, somewhere,
there in the middle of the book,
that young reflection of myself
ever turning the pages forward
as the sorcery of my remembrance
silently turns them back.

Windows

A Golden Shovel Poem* after L.M. Montgomery's
"The Little Gable Window"

Like an old friend, these pages turn and take me by
the hand, away to Prince Edward Island and the

distant space where I yet dream a little.
Maud's signal beckons from Anne's east gable,

calling through the years with her light in the window.
It blinks across time and space in flashes of

kindred code, a magnet, a beacon that
reaches this dreamer at a window in a Kansas cottage,

scribbling her own shimmery verses, sending them far,
droplets of light like dandelion seeds borne away.

---

*A poetic form created by Terrance Hayes in which the last words of each
line are the words, in order, from a line of poetry from an existing poem.

Dreamroom

"She wondered if old dreams could haunt rooms—if...something of her, intangible and invisible, yet nonetheless real, did not remain behind like a voiceful memory."
—*Anne of the Island*

She is there,
around some past corner,
that wide-eyed dreamer
who inhabited this room.
Her purply visions
populate the slant of light
dancing through the half-closed blind.
Her golden aspirations
chime in the window's memory
of countless summer breezes.
Her rosy ambitions
linger in the ghostly perfume
of the souls of wildflower bouquets.
She is yet here,
though every concrete inch
is desecrated by another.
Her spirit still sits
at a now-absent desk,
weaving verses out of airy voices,
writing herself indelibly
onto the unchanging pages
of her eternal space.

The Enchanted Forest

"And there was always the bend in the road!"
—Anne of Green Gables

It had been a long winter of short, dark days of feeling trapped inside an old farmhouse with no central heat and many expectations. I set out to explore that afternoon, never dreaming I would discover a magical realm hidden away on the hillside in the Flint Hills of Kansas. To others' eyes, it was just a stand of timber winding from the creek to the tallgrass prairie above, but to mine, it was an enchanted forest seemingly lifted from the plot of *Anne of Green Gables*. There was something mystical and not entirely worldly of this previously undiscovered space of winding paths and dancing shadows under a dome of intertwining redbud trees. Anything seemed possible there, my horizons seemed limitless, and my imagination soared to all the possibilities that awaited me on the other side of high school graduation in just a few weeks.

That spring, I spent many an afternoon walking, reading, and writing in the kingdom of my new discovery, which I promptly christened "The Enchanted Forest." There was meaning in a name like that, I decided, in keeping with the spirit of Anne Shirley. I relished every moment I could spend communing with my thoughts and hopes and dreams in all the secret nooks and corners I discovered. There, I felt no confines or limits to what I could and would do when I set off for college.

One day, school activities kept me from taking my walk until after dinner. I set off with my mother's stern warning not to stay out wandering around the countryside until after dark. I scrambled over the barbed wire fence that separated the fields from the Enchanted Forest and walked quickly, breathing in the cooling air and watching the waning light sift between the branches overhead. I hurried down my usual path, past the old limestone rocks wrenched from the fields above during the oil boom days, and up to the wide-open prairie. The tallgrass whispered quietly in the dusky breeze, and as I glanced out over the fields below, I realized how close it was to sunset. I should leave, avoid a scolding, but the palette of colors before me won out. Would Anne Shirley have turned her back on such a poem as that sunset sky? I asked myself. Of course not. So, I dropped to the ground and watched the sun rewrite the sky above the tender green of new fields and the swaying redbud trees. And I realized in that breath how truly small I was as I sat there looking down, across that wide expanse of landscape to the blurry line where earth met sky. I couldn't see beyond that distant horizon, yet I knew instinctively it was not a boundary but an invitation to dream about what lay beyond.

Today, as I turned the calendar to April 2020, I felt that same rush of hope, even in this time of anxiety, death, and despair. My memories flitted across the span of years to that long-ago April evening that still shapes my perspective, even in the midst of a pandemic. Looking back, as I do now, looking down, as I did then—that view from the fields still offers me a glimpse of my tiny place within a broader world and of the possibilities perhaps just out of sight beyond the horizon or around Anne Shirley's bend in the road. There, I dream of a point where we continue to look out, up, and about to take in the beauty in each day and each soul around us.

Lune

Wild cherry tree dreams
marble halls
from snowy blossoms.

Lands Without Mayflowers

"I'm so sorry for people who live in lands where there are no
Mayflowers…I think they must be the souls of the flowers that died last
summer and this is their heaven."
—*Anne of Green Gables*

Those who live in lands
without mayflowers
are to be pitied
their tragic deficit.
They know naught of
the sprinkling of stars
dreaming on emerald beds
among the rustlings
of an Island forest floor.
Their seeking hands
have never held
the blushing hope
of an impromptu bouquet.
They have never walked
the golden path
on reverent feet,
following Anne
through the blossoms of heaven,
weaving lacy visions
of the souls of summers past.

Violet Vale

purple brushstrokes stain
cool morning's hazy canvas
petals bow their heads

Shining Waters

Early morning light glints
in diamond heartbeats,
nostalgic flickers
like so many souls of falling stars
glimmering in the frosty dawn.
Ripples scatter golden patterns,
momentary glimpses
of other days,
simpler times,
forgotten dreams.
And in the hint
of the coming day,
I turn my face to taste
of new beginnings,
rising out of distant hills,
reflected in shining waters
before me,
within.

Wind and Stars and Fireflies

"Anne…felt that wind and stars and fireflies were all tangled up together into something unutterably sweet and enchanting."
—*Anne of Green Gables*

Tiny lanterns flicker
among the sweetness of the clover,
evening will-o'-the-wisps
tracing the pulse of summer
upon the canvas of white and green.
A puckish breeze rustles
the vision of leaves above,
purrs across the lane
distilling the song of June
into some undefinable fragrance.
The first pinpricks above peek out,
turning and preening,
admiring their twinkling reflection
in the field's constellation below.
And I breathe in this tangle
of wind and stars and fireflies,
endeavoring to unravel
the cipher of a summer dusk.

Octobers

"'I'm so glad I live in a world where there are Octobers. It would be terrible if we just skipped from September to November, wouldn't it?'"
—*Anne of Green Gables*

Octobers
may come and go—
some, a mosaic of
gold and crimson and bronze,
others, a drab swath
of dying summer.
But all are cloaked
in burnished perfection
for those with enough
scope for the imagination
to envision a world
bereft of
Octobers.

Sixku*

Inspired by Anne Shirley's sensibilities.

Gilded
leaves refract
fireflies' spirit light.

---

*Six-word poetic form inspired by a photograph; invented by Cendrine Marrouat

The Dream of a Fragrance

Inspired by Chapter XXXIII of *Anne of Green Gables*

White-ruffled curtains
dance in the essence
of an April evening breeze.
Lilacs on the sill
of the old farmhouse window
perfume the room
in twilight hues.
Hints of mellow sunlight
glint off the antique mirror,
a frame of reflected blossoms,
a youthful face,
visions of a hopeful future.
Even after so many seasons
have turned,
I still gaze at my image
poised on the threshold of life.
Each Proustian breath beckons,
filling all the me's
in all the mirrors
with the dream of a fragrance
recovering lost time.

Narcissus poeticus

"'Let's sit right down here among the narcissi…It looks as if the garden were carpeted with moonshine and sunshine combined.'"
—*Anne of Avonlea*

Fragrant blossoms reward
the patience of months.
Struggling against
the weight of the earth,
the elements,
and temperamental gods,
tender shoots arise,
white petals unfurl,
blank pages awaiting words.
The poets wrote of you,
Narcissus,
disdainful object
of Echo's affection,
lovely target of
Nemesis's revenge,
victim of your own beauty,
ultimately immortal
because of their verse.
Fleeting love,
fleeting vengeance,
fleeting life,
captured in enduring lines, for
this flower belongs
to the poets.
And I gaze
transfixed,
mesmerized,
reflected among them
in these dainty poems,
eternal lines
where Nemesis prevails,
Narcissus falls,
and Echo still whispers
on the wind.

The Souls of Good Violets

"Do you think amethysts can be the souls of good violets?"
—*Anne of Green Gables*

A tapestry of April dusks
reflects in gentle waves.
Flecks of light glint
off silver wings at evenfall,
glimpses beyond the curtain
into the heart of spring.
Tiny blossoms
hopeful,
brave,
defiant
carpet the shadows
of some timeless vale.
Alone at my window,
the last light plays
off the radiant twilight
and shimmery flight
encircling my finger,
the souls of good violets
of some eternal spring.

Once

"'Just now my garden is like faith—the substance of things hoped for. But bide a wee.'"
—*Anne's House of Dreams*

Once upon a spring
there were months
that brought new horrors
like other years brought flowers.

Sickness
death
fear
isolation
hate
blossomed
like so many weeds.

But a few hearty souls,
not even master gardeners,
refused to give in,
and trowels in hand,
they set to work
clearing out the old,
planting in the new,
daily toiling
for a better garden.

"But remember,"
they warned us
as we joined their efforts,
"the best and
most beautiful gardens
must be ever-tended."

A New Day

A Golden Shovel Poem after *Anne of Green Gables*

On the other side of this night lies tomorrow,
a sparkling morn of possibility that is
a blank slate upon which to write a
story, a poem, a song of golden rays and new
blossoms, a chance to start a fresh, clear day.
Though the night has shrouded hope with
scudding clouds, moonless sky, and no
stars sparkle to soften my glaring mistakes,
Anne-like, I still choose to believe in
the power of another dawn, following as it
guides me in the visions I dream yet.

Marilla Cuthbert

Something about her
hints of wells of humor
deep, but flowing.

Matthew Cuthbert

Pale as
sweet blossoms' lace
entwined o'er the White Way,
so too the final Presence on
his face.

Diana Barry

One bright sip
writes woe on friendship's pages
in currant ink.

The Opening Door

"…the door was flung open and in rushed Diana Barry."
—*Anne of Green Gables,* Chapter XVIII

Ice-encased branches hang,
like so many crystals,
still against a leaden sky.
Flickering firelight dances
across the frosty patterns
woven on the windowpanes.
My eyes trace the words
etched in time
as I sit in companionable silence
with my kindred spirits,
awaiting the possibility
that comes with
the opening door.

Gilbert Blythe

A slate
in anger cracked
as words in stormy hands
engrave a single name upon
his heart.

Dancing Wings

"Weeping may endure for a night but joy cometh in the morning."
—Psalm 30:5, as quoted by Anne Shirley in *Anne of the Island*

The sound of sunlight sparkles through the pane;
Bright birdsong ushers in another morn,
And dewy droplets whisper of the rain,
The jewels of a midnight tempest born.

The storm in inky lines proclaimed its tale,
And lightning slashed the sky in tattered shreds.
My fingers traced the scars in each last wail
And grasped for stars unraveled and in threads.

But darkness fades behind the chiming rays,
And silver ribbons swirl above the lane.
Songs weave the fabric of the coming days
And clothe with hope the remnants left of pain.

Outside, within, a tapestry of light,
And brilliant notes on dancing wings take flight.

In Hester Gray's Garden

A kindku* inspired by Chapter XLI "Love Takes up the Glass of Time"
—*Anne of the Island*

Garden paths wind to stillness,
moment paused in time.
Diamond sunbursts of the heart
glimmer in the dusk.
Love takes up its glass at last,
and whispering winds
speak of hope and memory.

---

*Kindku is a seven-line, 43-syllable form of found poetry created by Cendrine Marrouat and David Ellis. It includes seven words taken from the same page of a book or other source and uses them in the same order in which they were found, alternating between the first and last word of a line. For more information, visit https://abpoetryjournal.com/kindku-poetry-form/

Last Word

An ekphrastic poem inspired by *Elaine* by Sophie Gengembre Anderson
and *Anne of Green Gables* by L.M. Montgomery,
works inspired by Tennyson's "Lancelot and Elaine"

The Lily Maid always
speaks for herself,
no matter how unfortunate
she may be
floating soundlessly to Camelot
or sinking unromantically in Avonlea.

The frozen roar of the dragon
and silent mourning of the servant
flank Elaine's eternal statement,
written not in the letter
or namesake flower
clutched in her icy hands,
but in her pale defiance
of being discourteously
unheard.

So, too, the red-haired Lily Maid,
sinking en route to Camelot,
bequeaths her timeless testimony
written not in
practicalities,
the romantic rescue,
or her doomed performance,
but in her brave resistance
to externally-imposed
confines.

Anne's body,
like Elaine's,
their choices,
a final voice,
the last
word.

Thanks

Kindred Verse is a reality thanks to the support of some truly wonderful kindred spirits along the way. Your belief in this project has made it a reality.

Thank you to my publisher Blue Cedar Press and to Michael Poage and Gretchen Eick for working through the publishing process with me.

A special thanks to Jay Wallace for bringing my vision to life through this beautiful design. The cover, layout, and images all harken faithfully back to Anne and to myself.

Thank you to Kate Macdonald Butler, Dr. Elizabeth Rollins Epperly, and Dr. Kate Scarth for your support of my project.

To all the individuals around the globe who enthusiastically agreed to read the manuscript and write a promotional blurb: I am grateful for your time and interest in this collection.

Thanks to my supportive husband, PJ Vaske, for believing in my dreams and encouraging me along the way. Only a Gilbert-level husband would have suggested we honeymoon on Prince Edward Island.

My dog, Mozzie, deserves special thanks for sitting patiently at my feet while I wrote.

And to my bosom friend across the years, Lesley Sieger-Walls: Thank you for your friendship for "as long as the sun and the moon shall endure."

Acknowledgments

I would like to thank the following publications in which these pieces, sometimes in different versions, originally appeared.

"Looking for Anne: Postcard from Prince Edward Island" was published in *Cagibi*, vol. 8, no. 1, 2019.

"Windows" was published in *Journal of L.M. Montgomery Studies,* June 1, 2020, https://journaloflmmontgomerystudies.ca/vistas/Sellers/windows. CC BY 4.0 [https://creativecommons.org/licenses/by/4.0/].

"The Enchanted Forest" was published as "My Dream for What Lies Beyond" in *Daily Inspired Life*, April 15, 2020. https://dailyinspiredlife.com/dream-beyond-by-julie-a-sellers-inspiring-story/?fbclid=IwAR2SYlGIgzPH1h8hb3-5LurAgRbJ5xMFbaA4BQhesZmOefs76Re-RiTPbunQ

"A New Day," "Once," and "In Hester Gray's Garden" were published in *The Auroras & Blossoms PoArtMo Anthology,* edited by David Ellis and Cendrine Marrouat, Auroras & Blossoms, 2020.

About the Author

Julie A. Sellers was raised in the Flint Hills near the small town of Florence, Kansas. After living in several states and countries, Julie is happy to make her home in Atchison, Kansas, where she is an Associate Professor of Spanish at Benedictine College. Julie has published three academic books, and her creative prose and poetry have appeared in publications such as *Cagibi, Eastern Iowa Review, Wanderlust* and *Kansas Time + Place*. Julie was the Kansas Author's Club 2020 Prose Writer of the year. A lifelong fan of *Anne of Green Gables,* Julie regrets that her middle name is spelled without an "e."

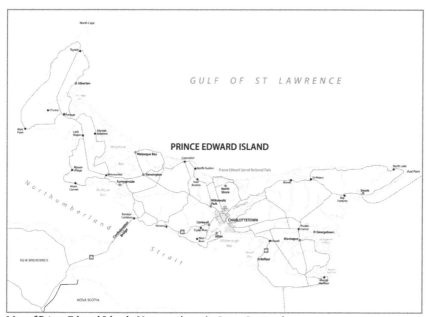

Map of Prince Edward Island - Vector road map by Rainer Lesniewski